The
Tundra

The
Tundra

Zachary Inseth

THE CHILD'S WORLD®, INC.

Library of Congress Cataloging-in-Publication Data
Inseth, Zachary.
The tundra / by Zachary Inseth.
p.   cm.
Includes index.
Summary: Questions and answers
introduce the appearance, location,
importance, and life of the tundra.
ISBN 1-56766-485-7 (smythe-sewn, library reinforced : alk. paper)
1. Tundras—Juvenile literature.
[1. Tundras—Miscellanea.]   I. Title.
GB571.I57   1998
551.45'3—dc21   97-34536
CIP
AC

Photo Credits

© Art Wolfe/Tony Stone Images: 2
© Beth Davidow: 23, 30
© Daniel J. Cox/Natural Exposures: 16
© 1994 Darrell Gulin/Dembinsky Photo Assoc. Inc: cover
© 1995 Darrell Gulin/Dembinsky Photo Assoc. Inc: 24. 29
© Greg Probst/Tony Stone Images: 10
© John Warden/Tony Stone Worldwide: 6, 19
© 1997 Rod Planck/Dembinsky Photo Assoc. Inc: 20
© Richard During/Tony Stone Images: 13
© Rosemary Calvert/Tony Stone Images: 26
© Stan Osolinski/Tony Stone Worldwide: 15
© Tom Walker/Tony Stone Worldwide: 9

On the cover...

Front cover: This Alaskan tundra is very colorful in the fall.
Page 2: This moose is walking across the quiet tundra.

Table of Contents

Chapter	Page
Welcome to the Tundra!	7
Where Is the Tundra Found?	8
What Does the Tundra Look Like?	11
How Did the Tundra Form?	12
What Are Tundra Winters Like?	17
What Are Tundra Summers Like?	18
What Plants Live on the Tundra?	21
What Animals Live on the Tundra?	25
Is the Tundra in Danger?	28
Index & Glossary	32

Welcome to the Tundra!

In the Far North there is a place that is full of changes. In the winter, the temperature drops to 70 degrees below zero. But in the summer, the Sun shines brightly—even at night! In this strange land, wolves howl and foxes play. There are even rabbits as white as snow. What kind of place is this? It's the beautiful tundra.

⇐ This tundra in Alaska is a beautiful place.

Where Is the Tundra Found?

If you were to travel from the middle part of the world to the north, you would see many changes. In the middle, the land is warm and wet. There are many tall trees and green plants. As you travel north, the weather gets colder. In the far north, the land becomes so cold that trees cannot grow.

Before you reach the icy region near the North Pole, you find a huge, flat, grassy land. This is the tundra. The tundra lies within the countries of Canada, Russia, Greenland, and the United States. The tundra is huge. In fact, it covers over 3 million square miles. That is about the size of the entire United States!

This tundra is wet and mushy during the summer. ⇒

What Does the Tundra Look Like?

The tundra looks a lot like a large grassland or prairie. It is big and flat and wide. Short grasses and mosses grow everywhere. The ground is often rough and mushy. The tundra has many small lakes and marshes, too.

In the northern part of the tundra, the ground is rocky. The weather is colder, and there are fewer plants. Here the tundra looks more like a cold, empty desert.

How Did the Tundra Form?

Long ago, much of the land in Europe and North America was frozen. Huge rivers of ice called **glaciers** moved slowly across the land. As they moved, the glaciers scraped and flattened the ground. For thousands of years, the glaciers moved across the tundra. Very slowly, they melted. In their path, the glaciers left huge, flat areas and bare rocks.

This glacier in Alaska is slowly changing the land around it. ⇒

Over time, a tiny plant called **lichen** started growing on the rocks. As the lichen grew, it crushed the rocks into dirt. This dirt was full of food, or **nutrients**, that helped other plants grow. Slowly, many types of plants began to grow on the tundra.

In the summer, these plants made the tundra the perfect place for many animals to find food. The tundra's open spaces were great for running and playing, too. Some animals liked the tundra so much, they began to live there all year long. Finally, after thousands of years, the empty tundra was full of living things.

Many different kinds of lichen are growing on these rocks. ⇒

What Are Tundra Winters Like?

As our planet Earth moves around the Sun, it tips in different directions. When the top of Earth tips away from the Sun, the Far North is covered in darkness. This is the tundra's wintertime.

Without warm sunlight, the tundra's winter is long, dark, and cold. Temperatures fall to 70 degrees below zero. The ground freezes and cold winds blow. Many tundra animals must travel south to find warmer weather and plants to eat. During the dark winter, the tundra is often a still and quiet place.

⇐ Without sunshine, this snow-covered tundra gets even colder.

What Are Tundra Summers Like?

After many months, the top of Earth tips toward the Sun again. Now summer comes to the tundra. The Sun shines on the frozen ground and warms the air. In fact, the Sun shines so much during the summer, it even shines at night! Soon the plants and mosses appear and flowers bloom. Birds and larger animals fill the green, grassy tundra. After the long winter, the tundra is now a warm and wonderful place.

These *fireweed* plants are growing in the tundra's warmer summer. ⇒

What Plants Live on the Tundra?

Summer on the tundra is only about three months long. With such a short summer, some of the tundra's ground stays frozen all year long. This frozen ground is called **permafrost**. If you could dig a hole in the tundra, the frozen permafrost would be very hard— even in the summer!

All plants have **roots** that grow under the ground. Roots gather water and nutrients the plants need to stay alive. Plants with roots that reach deep into the dirt can grow very tall. Most tundra plants are very short, though. They cannot grow deep roots because the permafrost is too hard. Plants such as grasses and mosses are the only plants that can survive on the tundra.

Lichen, *bearberry*, and other short plants grow easily on the tundra. ⇒

What Animals Live on the Tundra?

Since the tundra's winters are so long and cold, many animals live there only in the summer. During the summer they can find food to eat and places to run. But when the weather begins to get colder, many animals move south to warmer areas. This movement is called **migration**.

⇐ These *caribou* are migrating to warmer weather.

Birds, bears, and wild deer called *caribou* are tundra animals that migrate south for the winter. When summer returns, they migrate back to the tundra to eat and play.

But some animals are able to spend their whole lives on the tundra—even the winters! They have bodies or ways of living that help them stay alive in the cold. Most have thick coats of fur to help them stay warm. Arctic rabbits, wolves, foxes, and musk-oxen all live happily on the frozen tundra.

⇐ *Arctic foxes* like this one spend the whole winter on the tundra.　　27

Is the Tundra in Danger?

Until recently, very few people have lived on the tundra. It is just too cold! The plants and animals of the tundra have lived undisturbed for thousands of years. But now more people are beginning to move to the tundra. Many want to bring noisy machines that frighten the animals and pollute the air.

Noisy machines would frighten animals like this caribou. ⇒

The tundra is a very special type of land area, or **environment**. Many of its plants and animals do not live anywhere else in the world. If the tundra environment is destroyed, its plants and animals will disappear, too.

If we protect the tundra from the effects of machines and cities, its beautiful plants, land, and animals will be around for many years to come.

Glossary

environment (en–VY–run–ment)
An environment is the land, water, plants, and animals that make up a certain type of area. The tundra is one kind of environment.

glaciers (GLAY–sherz)
Glaciers are huge sheets of ice that move very slowly across the land. Long ago, glaciers covered the tundra.

lichen (LIE–ken)
Lichen are tiny plants that can live on bare rocks. Lichen were the first plants to grow on the tundra.

migration (my–GRAY–shun)
A migration is a journey animals take from one place to another. Many tundra animals migrate south for the winter.

nutrients (NOO–tree–ents)
Nutrients are food and vitamins that plants and animals need to live. Plants get their nutrients from the soil.

permafrost (PER–muh–frost)
Permafrost is a layer of ground that always stays frozen. The tundra has a great deal of permafrost.

roots (ROOTS)
Roots are the parts of a plant that live underground. The roots absorb water and nutrients from the soil.

Index

animals, 7, 14, 17-18, 25, 27

appearance, 8, 11

human development of, 28

environment, 31

formation, 12, 14

lichen, 14

location, 8

permafrost, 21

plants, 22

protection, 31

summers, 18, 21

winters, 17